THE MONI & CHRIS ADVENTURES™

BLACK BH HISTORY EDITION

★ ★ MONI & CHRIS GO TO THE ★ ★

RODEO

BY: MONICA FORTSON & CHRISTOPHER FORTSON

ILLUSTRATED BY CALVIN REYNOLDS

MW00946571

The Moni & Chris Adventures

Moni & Chris Go To The Rodeo

Copyright © 2020 Monica Fortson & Christopher Fortson

All Rights Reserved

This is a work of fiction.

All rights reserved. This book or any portion thereof may not be reproduced, distributed, or transmitted in any form or by any means, including photocopying, recording, or other electronic or mechanical methods, without the express written permission of the publisher except in the case of brief quotations embodied in critical reviews and certain other noncommercial uses permitted by copyright law.

For permissions requests, write to the publisher, addressed "Attention: Permissions Coordinator," at the address below.

Printed in the United States of America

ISBN: 978-1-953497-11-6 (Paperback)

ISBN: 978-1-953497-12-3 (Digital)

Library of Congress Control Number: 2021903118

Published by Cocoon to Wings Publishing

7810 Gall Blvd, #311

Zephyrhills, FL 33541

www.CocoontoWingsBooks.com

(813) 906-WING (9464)

Illustrations and Interior layout design by Calvin Reynolds/ Concepts Redefined, LLC

Cocoon to Wings
PUBLISHING

MONI & CHRIS™ GO TO THE RODEO

BY: MONICA FORTSON & CHRISTOPHER FORTSON

ILLUSTRATED BY CALVIN REYNOLDS

The Fortson family was just sitting down for dinner. "Did you know your mom was a real-life cowgirl?" Moni's dad asked.

4

"Really? A cowgirl?" both Moni and
Chris replied in disbelief.
They had never seen her around a
horse let alone actually riding one.

As their mom placed a basket of fresh baked rolls on the table, she informed her children, "Growing up at the Hightower Stables and the Diamond "L" Ranch; your mom not only rode horses, but barrel raced, too."

Moni and Chris were fascinated by this
new information about their mom.
"Is that why you wear cowboy boots?"
asked Chris.

Moni, being the older sister,
explained to her younger brother,
"Mom is a girl like me.
So, they are called cow **GIRL** boots."

Moni's dad chuckled. She sure did have a whole bunch of personality.
"Well, after your dad blesses the food, I'll tell you all about your grandma."
The Fortsons all bowed their heads as Moni and Chris' dad blessed the food.

"Your grandma was Verna Hightower
and her nickname was "Boots."
She was the first African American female
to compete in barrel racing at the Houston
Livestock Show and Rodeo back in 1969.
She was a great inspiration."

**Their mom went on to share that when
she was younger, the Diamond L was
one of the few places in Houston
where African Americans could
compete in professional rodeos.**

12

"Mom," Chris mumbled with
food in his mouth, "Who started it?
Can we visit the Diamond L? Was it fun?
Did you ever own a horse of your own?"

His mother laughed.
"Slow down Chris.
No talking with food
in your mouth,"
she replied.

For the entire dinner,
Mrs. Fortson smiled with joy while
sharing childhood memories about her
mom, Verna "Boots" Hightower,
and their home across the pasture
from the Diamond L.

When dinner was over,
Moni and Chris were so inspired.
Moni imagined herself as a
cowgirl, and Chris imagined
himself as a cowboy.
Rodeos, horses, boots, and barns
filled their dreams.

16

Moni and Chris were suddenly awakened.
"Rise and shine y'all! These horse stalls aren't
going to clean themselves,"
hollered a mysterious woman standing
in the doorway.

"Y'all get on up. Wash your face and brush your
teeth. Your grandfather is waiting for you,"
the lady instructed as she walked away.

Chris walked to the bedroom door and looked around. "I think we are in Houston," he told Moni. Moni jumped out of bed and raced to the bedroom window. When she peeked out....

20

"Horses! Chris, we aren't just in Houston.
We're at Grandma Boots and Grandpa Ted's!"
Chris ran and joined his sister looking out the window.
They could see their grandparents' barn and horses.
Moni and Chris were excited.

"Y'all ready to help turn the horses into the pasture and clean some stalls?" Moni and Chris turned to see their grandpa Ted smiling at them.

"Grab some breakfast and I'll meet you two in the barn." Grandpa Ted chuckled.

After getting dressed, Moni and Chris
grabbed breakfast and raced to the barn.

When they entered the barn, Moni and Chris were greeted by their two cousins, Dede and Gregory.

"Glad y'all could finally join us.
We already cleaned out three stalls." Dede said.
"Yea, it's about time!" laughed her
brother, Gregory, as he walked up.

After all the chores were done,
Grandma Boots told everyone to gather
around; she had an announcement.

"Next week I will be competing in the
Houston Livestock Show and Rodeo!"

"I thought you already did that?"
Chris questioned.
"He's just joking!" Moni quickly
interjected.

Moni whispered to Chris,
"We must be in 1969!
Which means we are about to
see history being made."

Moni and Chris helped their grandmother
set up the barrels in the practice arena.

"Barrels number 1 and 2 need to be 90 feet apart.
And barrel number 3 needs to be centered
105 feet from barrels 1 and 2."
Verna instructed as she mounted her horse.
Moni and Chris spent the remainder of the
week helping their grandmother practice.
They were overjoyed about the upcoming event.

When the big day arrived,
Verna stared into the crowd with excitment.
"Today, I change history.
"Tomorrow, you keep history alive."

**Moni looked up at her grandma wondering what
she meant, but before she could ask,
Verna was on her way to the starting gates.**

Moni and Chris eagerly listened as the announcer introduced their grandmother. "Now riding into the arena on her horse, King, Verna "Boots" Hightower!"

Off she went!

Verna turned the first barrel.

Then the second and third barrels.

She quickly raced to the finish line.

It was over. In less than 16 seconds,
Moni and Chris had seen the color barrier
broken and history made.
Black Rodeo was changed forever.

"BOOTS"

Verna Lee Booker Hightower
June 26, 1930-August 1970

Verna Lee Hightower was born on June 26, 1930 in the small town of Spring, Texas. Early in life, she was nicknamed "Boots" because of her love for horses and the outdoors. However, she began riding and training horses regularly after her marriage to Ted Hightower.

Training tenaciously on the barrels both morning and night, Verna was a vibrant personality who gained a reputation as a fearless rider. Bedecked in her tailor-made cowgirl apparel, Verna never slowed down when approaching the barrels.

The Diamond L Ranch rodeo arena in Houston (where she and Ted made their home) was renowned for championship competition among Black Cowboys and Cowgirls from around the United States.

There, Verna was recognized for her excellent Cowgirl talent, and she became one of the Diamond L Ranch rodeo's most competitive riders. On the Black Rodeo Circuit, Verna competed on the national level in Okmulgee and Henrietta, Oklahoma, as well as in Simonton and Pasadena, Texas. In addition to winning numerous first place awards in barrel racing on her horse "King," she also became the "poster girl" for locally produced rodeos.

Verna and Ted taught their six children a healthy respect for ranch animals and for riding. The youngest daughter, Dee Dee, started riding as a toddler and won or placed in a number of barrel racing competitions prior to her sudden death. Verna and her husband, Ted, and son, Gerald, received prize ribbons for their two horses (Glamour and King) in the "Western Pleasure" event at the 1969 Houston Livestock Show and Rodeo in the Astrodome. Verna and Ted were proud owners of several horses which they trained for competition in barrel racing and for cutting and showing.

The family was well known for being the first African-American family listed as trainers and owners of livestock shown in the Houston Livestock Show and Rodeo.

Verna made exemplary contributions to the Western Heritage through participating in various rodeo activities. She was also the first of her race to become a member of the Girl's Rodeo Association (GRA). With this membership, Verna was entitled to participate in the larger rodeos and to earn points qualifying her to compete nationally. Other memberships included the National Colored Rodeo Association (N.C.R.A.), and the Southwestern Rodeo Association.

Verna was the first African-American woman to participate in the Barrel Racing competition in the Houston Livestock Show and Rodeo during the years of 1969 and 1970.

Verna's death in August, 1970 came much too soon for all that knew her. Her love for horses and her athletic cowgirl abilities are still talked about among many African-American cowboys and cowgirls today.

Her photo still appears on some rodeo posters in Texas.

Verna was inducted into the Multicultural Western Heritage Museum Hall of Fame, Fort Worth, TX., in 2007. In 2015 the Houston Livestock Show and Rodeo Black Heritage Committee established the Verna Lee Booker Hightower Award to be presented to honorees at the committee's annual Western Gala.

Indeed, Verna Lee Hightower was a pioneer among the Western Heritage, and her courageous spirit opened doors for the many rodeo athletes of color that have participated in the Houston Livestock Show and Rodeo.

About The Author

A Seattle, Washington native,
Monica Fortson now calls Houston, Texas home.
Her first co-authorship, Fearless Faith, was published in 2018.
In 2020, Monica turned her love of writing, traveling, and
educating youth into an imaginative and fun-filled children's
series. Partnering with her brother, Christopher Fortson, The
Moni and Chris Adventures was created.
Outside of children's books, Monica shares her life
experiences through inspirational speaking.
When she is not creating, Monica spends her free time with
her family, horses and dogs. She is the founder and CEO of
The Fortson Group, LLC
and a member of Delta Sigma Theta Sorority Incorporated.

About The Illustrator

Calvin Reynolds is a professional
illustrator/graphic designer and award-winning children's book
author from Tampa Bay, Florida.
His desire to inspire children has led him to create
and illustrate stories that capture their imagination and foster a
love of reading and art.
See more of Calvin's illustrations at jaycethebee.com

Made in the USA
Columbia, SC
21 July 2021

42197964R00022